About the Book

Saucy was going to have puppies. The Brown family didn't know *when* she would have them but they wanted to make sure *where* she would have them. Each one tried to find just the right spot. Roger found a soft place but it didn't please Saucy. Jenny found a dark place but Saucy didn't like that either. Even a warm place wasn't right.

Then Saucy disappeared. The Browns and all their neighbors searched and searched. It was no use. No one could find the secret place that Saucy had found for her puppies.

Weekly Reader Children's Book Club *presents*

SAUCY

by Martha McKeen Welch

ILLUSTRATED BY UNADA

Coward-McCann, Inc.   New York

Library of Congress Catalog Card Number: 68-18826
PRINTED IN THE UNITED STATES OF AMERICA

Weekly Reader Children's Book Club Edition
Primary Division

FOR CLARA with love
and, of course,
FOR MARDI and PETER

Saucy was going to have puppies. No one in the Brown family knew exactly *when* she was going to have them, but at least they could make sure *where* she was going to have them.

"A soft place," Roger said, "and near me."

He put a soft blanket on the floor beside his bed. Saucy looked at it and sniffed it a little, but then she went away.

"A dark place," said Jenny, who was younger. "And near me."

She put the blanket in her closet. But Saucy wouldn't go near it.

"A warm place, then," Roger said. He got a big box from the garage. He cut out one end to make an entrance, leaving a few inches of cardboard at the bottom so the puppies could not fall out. Jenny lined it with clean newspapers and they put it in the kitchen near the stove.

Saucy perked up her fuzzy ears and jumped in. She rumpled the newspapers to make a nest, then settled down. At last she was satisfied!

But not for long. After a few minutes Saucy mussed up the papers some more and jumped out. They couldn't make her get in again.

"What's wrong?" Roger wondered. "We've tried everything. A soft place, a dark place, a warm place. What else could she possibly want?"

That night after dinner, Mr. Brown was reading the paper, Jenny was helping her mother dry the dishes, and Roger was watching a squirrel out of the window.

Saucy was at the door. She wanted to go out. Roger and Jenny went with her.

The moon was rising, so the children climbed up in their tree house to watch it. Gradually the sky grew dark and the moon turned from orange to yellow. It was time for bed.

Roger called Saucy, but Saucy didn't come. Jenny called, too. They went all around the house calling.

"Get on your sweaters," Mrs. Brown said, "and we'll look with flashlights."

They looked under every bush near the house. Roger looked in the garage and Jenny looked in the tool shed. All of them kept calling. Once they heard a scratchy sound in the dry leaves, but it was only a bird.

Finally they had to give up and go to bed. But Roger couldn't get to sleep. What if the puppies were born outside? Would they catch cold? Or would some animal hurt them? What if it should start to rain, or even snow? There was no soft, dark, warm place outside.

Twice he ran to the window in the middle of the night when he heard a dog bark in the distance. He could see quite well in the moonlight. The trees made long, skinny shadows, but he couldn't see Saucy. Once an owl hooted, which was scary, and Roger noticed how cold it was.

The next morning Mrs. Brown phoned all the neighbors. They said they would help. Thirteen children came to look. Everyone was calling Saucy. They scattered in all directions.

Sammy Ross looked around the old chicken house across the field. The milkman asked at each house as he made his deliveries. The grocer told everyone who came in his store. And Mrs. Brown called the radio station and had an announcement put on the Pet Parade for lost animals.

But no one found Saucy.

Then someone came running. It was Sammy Ross. He was shouting, *"Follow me!"* and everybody ran — past the post office and the bus stop, across the Jones' back yard, and down to the old mill.

"She's there, I know, I heard her!" Sammy cried. "Listen!"

They all stopped and were quiet. Yes, they could hear something rustling behind the old water wheel. They stood very still. No one made a sound as Roger got down on his knees to look.

Suddenly a small head poked out quite near him, and then, quickly, a muskrat scurried for the water and disappeared with a splash.

Saucy was not there.

More and more people joined the search: the minister and his wife, the postman, two policemen, a fat nursemaid, an old man with a white beard and a cane. Everyone wanted to find Saucy, but no one did.

Another long night went by. As soon as it
started to get light outside, Roger put on his jacket
over his pajamas, took the flashlight, and went
quietly downstairs. He couldn't wait another minute.
Maybe if he went alone he could find Saucy.

Just then he heard a familiar scratching.
He rushed to open the back door.
   Saucy ran in!

She looked much thinner. Roger was sure her puppies had been born. She lapped up every drop of water in her bowl, then asked to go right out again. Roger knew she would go back to her puppies, so he opened the door and followed.

At first Saucy turned around to make sure Roger was coming, but then she started to run faster without looking back. Roger couldn't keep up. Saucy sped beyond the garden and was gone! Somewhere across the field. Near the old chicken house? Roger didn't know where Saucy was.

Roger ran across the field. It was the right direction. When he reached the old chicken house, he started to call softly. He looked through the broken windows and walked all around the chicken house. Then he knelt down and looked underneath. The floor was raised a few inches from the ground, so he could see through to the other side, but it was dark in the middle. He beamed his light quickly around, but he couldn't see anything.

Roger turned to go when he felt something rub-
bing against his leg.

Saucy!

She wagged her tail and watched to be sure
Roger was looking. Then she squeezed under the
chicken house.

Roger lay down with his face on the ground and shined the flashlight under the floor again. There was Saucy! Right in the middle where he couldn't possibly reach her. At least not without help.

Roger ran to get his family. "Wake up! Wake up!" he yelled.

Jenny got a basket. Mrs. Brown got a Turkish towel and filled a hot-water bottle. Mr. Brown got a saw and a hammer. Roger got a leash and led the way.

They opened the rickety door of the chicken house and found a spot that Roger thought was just above Saucy.

"We'll have to break through the floor," Mr. Brown said.

"I can hear them! They're alive!" Jenny cried. And sure enough, they heard little squeaky sounds coming up from under the floor.

Mr. Brown sawed through the floorboards just a little to one side. Then he yanked a board up with his hammer. When the opening was big enough, they all looked down underneath.

There they were! One, two, three, four, *five* perfect little puppies! All warm and safe and dusty.

Saucy had made a hole and filled it with leaves. It was soft, and dark, and warm, just like the places Roger and Jenny had fixed for her in the house.

Suddenly Roger grinned. There *was* one thing he hadn't thought of. One more thing Saucy had wanted. Carefully he picked up the puppies, one by one, and put them in the basket on top of the hot-water bottle. Mrs. Brown wrapped the towel around them and they hurried back to the house.

Roger put the box in the cellar next to the furnace. Saucy got right into it, and Roger placed the babies beside her. Jenny brought a bowl of warm milk and some of Saucy's favorite dog food, and Roger watched as Saucy ate, and drank, and wagged her tail.

She looked up at him, and Roger knew he had been right. He had fixed her a place like the one she had chosen — soft, and dark, and warm...

and

private.

Besides all that, Saucy was *HOME!*

The Author

Born in Easton, Pennsylvania, MARTHA McKEEN WELCH says that she was "constantly surrounded by pets of all kinds — cats, dogs, ponies, raccoons, skunks, honey bears, monkeys, and parrots."

Mrs. Welch studied in Europe and has traveled extensively in the United States and Europe. She has studied art and design and photography.

Mrs. Welch now lives in Westchester County, New York, with her husband and two children and is "once more surrounded by pets."

The Artist

UNADA lives in Philadelphia, Pennsylvania, where she works as a freelance illustrator. Born in Rochester, New York, she attended the school of art at Syracuse University, where she was graduated *magna cum laude*. She has worked in an advertising agency and was the staff artist for the Lutheran Board of Parish Education in Philadelphia.